The girl who talks to animals

Magic Molly

The Shy Piglet

HOLLY WEBB

Illustrated by Erica Jane Waters

SCHOLASTIC

First published in the UK in 2011 by Scholastic Children's Books
An imprint of Scholastic Ltd
Euston House, 24 Eversholt Street
London, NW1 1DB, UK
Registered office: Westfield Road, Southam, Warwickshire, CV47 0RA
SCHOLASTIC and associated logos are trademarks
and/or registered trademarks of Scholastic Inc.

Text copyright © Holly Webb, 2011
Illustration copyright © Erica Jane Waters, 2011

The rights of Holly Webb and Erica Jane Waters to be identified as
the author and illustrator of this work have been asserted by them.

Cover illustration © Erica Jane Waters 2011

ISBN 978 1 407 12167 3

Printed by CPI Bookmarque, Croydon, CR0 4TD
Papers used by Scholastic Children's Books are made from
wood grown in sustainable forests.

1 3 5 7 9 10 8 6 4 2

www.scholastic.co.uk/zone

For Tabitha, who will be able
to read it all by herself

Chapter One

School Trip

"Don't forget your packed lunch, Molly!" Her dad, Sam, grabbed it off the kitchen table and passed it to her.

"Oops, sorry, Dad, I'm just so excited!" Molly gave her dad a quick hug, and he laughed.

"You'll have a brilliant time. Now, hurry up, or you'll miss the coach." He glanced at the kitchen clock. "And I'm going to be late for early morning surgery. Tell me all about it at teatime!"

1

"Bye, Dad!" Molly dashed out into the yard, where her mum, Jo, and her little sister Kitty were waiting for her, and her dad hurried out after her, making for the buildings on the other side of the yard. Molly's dad was a vet, and he ran his own surgery, Larkfield Vets. Molly loved that they lived so close to the surgery – it meant that she got lots of chances to go and visit the animals, and she was sure that she was going to be a vet herself when she was older.

"I'm so looking forward to this!" Molly told her best friend, Alice, as they sat down together on the coach. "I looked on the Blossom Farm website. They have some gorgeous animals; really, really tiny ponies, and goats that you can feed, and an enormous rabbit, and..."

Alice laughed. "I can see why you wanted to go there. It sounds like a dream place for you, Molly."

Molly nodded. "It's only been open for a few weeks. I asked Mum if she could take me and Kitty, but she and Dad are just too busy at the moment." Molly smiled. She adored her dad, and she was really proud that he was a vet and spent all his time caring for animals, but he did work very hard! "One of the nurses has gone off to train to be a vet herself now, and they haven't got anyone to replace her yet. So Mum's filling in. Grandad's been looking after us."

"I love your grandad," Alice said.

Molly grinned. "It's extra good because even though Grandad loves cooking, he only likes making cakes, so he gives us fish fingers or sausages for tea every day, and then cake for pudding. It's fab."

"Why would we want to go to a stupid farm?" somebody muttered behind Molly and Alice. "I'd much rather have gone to the chocolate factory. Farms are for girls."

Molly rolled her eyes and mouthed, "Ben!" at Alice.

Alice nodded disgustedly. Ben, who was in the seat behind them, was always grumpy about something. He was mean

to everyone,
and Alice really
didn't like him,
as he'd teased
her loads when
she'd started at
Larkfield School
a few weeks
before. She was
quite a shy person,
and she'd found
moving schools
really difficult.

Molly turned round
and glared at him. "Farms are not just for
girls! Everyone likes animals, and you're
just being difficult on purpose."

Alice shrank down in her seat a little.
"Don't annoy him!" she whispered
urgently. "He'll be horrible."

Molly only sniffed. "I'd like to see him try! He's only nasty to people who don't fight back, Alice."

Alice shuddered. "I'm not good at fighting back. Let's not talk about him. Did Kitty mind that you were going to the farm? Does she want to go too?"

Molly nodded. "Yes, but I'd rather go with you and everyone from school. Kitty's awful at things like that. She just wants to stroke one animal the whole time, and you can't make her move. We went to the zoo once, and Mum had to spend the entire time with her in front of the giraffes because if we tried to make her go anywhere else she screamed."

Alice giggled. "Sometimes I wish I had a little sister, though. Kitty's really cute."

Molly wrinkled her nose. "Only if you don't have to live with her, I think. Oh, I suppose she is really. But little sisters can be very annoying. I'd rather have a pony, like you."

Alice smiled. "Silver's the nicest pony ever..." she murmured happily.

Molly smiled out of the coach window. She was the only person who knew that, really, Alice's pony Silver wasn't a pony at all. He was a unicorn who had been stolen away by poachers. He was staying with Alice for now, and he let her ride him. Molly had helped Silver get special silver horseshoes so his magic wouldn't fade.

Molly was very good at helping animals –
especially magical ones!

*I wonder if there are any magical animals at
Blossom Farm?* Molly thought to herself.

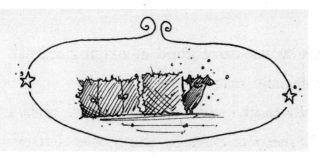

Chapter Two

Hidden Magic

"Ah, look, those chickens have got little furry hats on!" Molly giggled.

"This poster says they're called Poland chickens," Alice read off the board next to the chickens' run. "Aren't they cute? Oh, that's weird. It says they're calmer than most chickens because they can't see with all those feathers over their eyes!" She wrinkled her nose. "I think I'd be *more* worried if I had a hat pulled down over my eyes all the time, not less."

One of the Poland chickens stepped delicately over to the edge of its run and eyed Molly with its head on one side. It had to peer through the feathers, its eyes bright and sparkly and curious.

Molly crouched down, and the chicken  rubbed its beak against her fingers gently.

Alice sighed. "I can't believe you've just met that chicken and it's behaving like you've known it for ever!"

Molly smiled, and gave a little shrug. "I've just got a magic touch. My dad always says so. I bet she'd do it for you too. Try and stroke her."

Alice stretched out her hand a little nervously, but the chicken made a soft clucking noise and stroked its feathery topknot against Alice's fingers.

"Oh, it's so soft," Alice whispered.

"She really likes you – look, she's gone all cuddly!" Molly laughed.

The chicken was rubbing its head against Alice now and cooing, and the rest of the flock was gathering around Molly. Bella and Lucy, two of the other girls from Molly and Alice's class, came up behind them and laughed. "Wow. Animals really love you, Molly," Bella said admiringly.

"Have you seen the pigs? There's some really tiny ones in one of the pens over there." Lucy pointed over to the other side of the big yard.

"Oh, I love pigs." Molly gave the

chickens a last pat, and Alice scattered some grain from the little bag they'd been given when they arrived. The chickens scuttled off, pecking eagerly, and the girls headed round the corner to see the piglets. They were old enough to have stopped feeding from their mother and were in a big pen on their own, all rooting around in a muddy patch in the middle.

Molly giggled. "Look at their curly tails – piglets always make me laugh."

Alice leaned on the edge of the pen. "Do you think pigs have lovely soft skin? My mum has a jar of really expensive mud stuff that she puts on her face, and just look at those piglets. They're covered in it!"

Molly frowned. "I don't think that looks like very expensive mud, Alice. Hey, what's Ben doing over there?"

On the other side of the little path through the animals, Ben was standing on the bottom rung of the railings, reaching over into one of the pens.

"He's got a stick!" Molly said, sounding horrified.

"He isn't trying to hurt one of the animals, is he?" Alice squeaked in shock.

"He'd better not be!" Molly bounced

up and ran over to Ben. "Hey! What are you doing?"

"Nothing!" Ben snapped. "And what's it to you, anyway?"

"I'm not going to let you get away with poking a stick at some poor little creature," Molly said, standing with her hands on her hips.

"I wasn't!" Ben shouted back.

"We saw you!"

"I just wanted – oh, never mind!" Ben flung the stick on to the ground and stormed off, vanishing around the corner of the pens.

"He is so horrible!" Alice came up to Molly. "You were really brave to yell at him like that. What was he trying to poke that stick at?"

"I'm not sure." Molly crouched down to look through the bars. "There's nothing in there that I can see. Ben's probably terrified whatever it is."

"Tell you what, you see if you can cheer it up, and I'll go after Ben, just to make sure he's not hurting anything else," Alice suggested. "And if he is..." She sighed. "Well, I'll tell Mrs Moffat, I suppose."

Molly gave her a hug. "You'll get over being scared of him. If I hadn't been here, I bet you would have stopped him hurting whoever's in this pen."

Alice looked uncertain. "Maybe. See you in a bit, anyway."

Molly looked back into the pen, waiting patiently for the creature inside to show itself. She could feel that there was someone there, and she suspected it might be someone special. There was a fizzing, glittering feeling in the air; Molly could almost taste it.

"Hello!" she whispered.

Nothing moved. But Molly could see a very tiny patch of pink behind the straw bale at the back of the pen. A patch that could just about be the tip of an ear.

"Hello!" she tried again.

The pink patch twitched, just a little.

Molly settled herself more comfortably by the side of the pen and prepared to wait. Whatever was hiding behind that bale would come out when it was good and ready, she decided. Being patient was one of the things that made her so good with animals – it was nothing to do with magic, she just didn't mind waiting.

The pink patch twitched again, and then a small pink nose peeped out around the hay bale, followed by a curious black eye.

Someone behind Molly laughed, and she glanced round in surprise.

One of the girls from the farm – Molly could tell by her blue uniform – was standing behind her. "You should be very honoured," she told Molly, smiling. "We've actually named that piglet Mouse, because he's so shy. He never normally comes out of his hiding place."

"Why is he so shy?" Molly asked.

"We really don't know, poor little pig. We had to move him out of the pen with his brothers and sisters – he kept trying to hide himself away because he doesn't seem to like noise or mess. He got quite upset. See if you can get him to come out." The girl smiled and walked on, and Molly stared back into the pen. A shy piglet. She had never heard of such a thing.

Once the farm girl's footsteps had died away, the pretty pink nose crept back around the edge of the hay bale, and when Molly didn't move, it came out a little more, so that Molly could see all of the little pig's head – then his body, and then at last a whole piglet was standing pressed against the hay bale, trembling a little.

"Please don't be scared!" Molly whispered, and then she gasped as the piglet began to walk delicately towards her, carefully avoiding the muddy puddles in his pen.

He was spotless. Perfectly clean and perfectly pink, with long, sandy-white eyelashes. Molly had never seen a cleaner, prettier little pig.

Chapter Three

Meeting Mouse

The piglet walked towards her, and Molly smiled with delight. Even his little trotters looked polished. Very slowly, Molly reached out a hand, to see if Mouse would let her stroke him. He ducked his head next to the railings, and she stroked his ears. They were velvet soft, covered with fine downy hair, and as she touched him a thrill of magic ran into her fingers and seemed to dance through her bones. He *was* magical! She had thought he must be.

Hello, he said shyly. His voice was a
quiet little whisper in Molly's head, as
he looked at her sideways under his long
eyelashes.

Hello, Molly said back, still smiling.
Everything about the little pig made her
feel happy. *Are you all right? Ben – that
boy – he didn't hurt you?*

Oh, no! Mouse shook his head. *The*

stick wasn't long enough to reach me. And I don't think he was trying to hurt me, either. He wanted to talk to me, I think. I just wasn't quite brave enough to come out and see, he added sadly.

Molly nodded slowly. She really had thought Ben was trying to poke something with the stick, but she supposed she could have been wrong.

"Molly!" Molly jumped. It was Alice calling. "Molly, we have to go and watch the milking now, Mrs Moffat sent me to fetch you. Oh, what a sweet little pig!"

But all of a sudden, the piglet wasn't there any more. He had vanished back behind his hay bale, as soon as he had seen Alice.

"Gosh, you really are shy," Molly murmured.

Alice stood there looking guilty. "I

didn't mean to scare him away," she told Molly sadly.

"I don't think it was you," Molly told her. "He's just super-shy. Even worse than you!" She leaned down close to the railings again. "I have to go, Mouse, but I promise I'll come back later!"

But after the milking demonstration, Mrs Moffat said that it was time for everyone to get back on the coach. *But I promised Mouse!* Molly thought in horror. *I have to go back and see him.* Before anyone could stop her, she ducked quickly away from her group, running to hide by a pile of hay bales. Then she darted one glance back behind her, to see if anyone had noticed her run off. Ben was staring in surprise round the side of the coach. She stared back at him, waiting for him to yell for Mrs Moffat, but he didn't. She raised one hand in a startled, thankful wave, and he nodded and popped back again.

Molly was too busy worrying about Mouse, and about what Mrs Moffat would say when she got back, to worry about Ben now.

"Mouse! Mouse!" she hissed as she flung herself down the passage where his pen was. "I have to go back to school now, but I promise I'll come back for a proper visit and see you. Mouse! Are you there?"

The little pink nose appeared cautiously

around the hay bale, and Mouse trotted forward. *Come back soon!* he told Molly silently. *I need your help, to make me friendly like the others. Please, I hate being so shy!*

Molly nodded. "I will, I promise. But I have to go, I'm going to get into trouble."

Molly raced back to the coach, hoping that Mrs Moffat hadn't noticed she'd gone. But Mrs Moffat was standing by the coach door, worriedly counting the line of children. "Someone's missing," she was saying to Miss Benham, their classroom assistant.

"It's Molly," several helpful voices told her, and Molly sighed and slunk up to the teacher.

"I'm not missing, I'm here!" she said brightly.

"Molly! Where on earth have you been?" Mrs Moffat said crossly. "Really,

25

I wouldn't have expected someone as sensible as you to disappear."

Luckily, the coach driver was starting to look a bit impatient, so Mrs Moffat simply sighed and waved Molly on to the coach with the others.

"Where did you go?" Alice whispered to her curiously as they climbed the steps.

"Just to see Mouse the piglet again. I wanted to say goodbye to him..." Molly glanced at Alice, wondering if she'd think that was silly. But she only smiled and nodded.

As Alice sat down, Molly leant over the seat behind them to talk to Ben.

"Thanks for not telling Mrs Moffat I ran off."

"That's OK," said Ben. "Was the piglet all right? I didn't mean to hurt him."

Molly nodded thoughtfully. "How did you know it was a piglet?" she asked.

Ben looked at her in surprise. "I don't know. I didn't actually see it, I really wanted to, but..." He blinked. "I suppose there must have been a notice saying so."

Molly smiled. "Probably." But she knew there hadn't been. So how had Ben known that Mouse was there?

All the way back home from school, and all that evening, Molly wondered if there

was something she could do to help
Mouse. Molly hadn't done a lot of magic
on her own, but maybe she could do a
spell? An anti-shyness spell, if there was
such a thing? She smiled to herself. If she
managed to find one, she could use it on
Alice too. *And Ben*, a little voice in her
head added, and she blinked in surprise.
Ben didn't need a spell to stop him being
shy! He was the loudest, nastiest person in
their class! Although he hadn't been that
bad today. He hadn't told on Molly, and
Mouse had said he wasn't being mean,
like she'd thought.

"Were there zebras? Molly!" Kitty
tugged at her arm impatiently. Molly
had been thinking to herself the whole
time and not answering her little sister's
questions about the farm. "Zebras!"

Molly smiled and shook her head. "No.

But there was an alpaca – a thing that looks a bit like a camel."

"Oh," Kitty said sadly. "I like zebras best."

"You'd love the animals at the farm," Molly promised her. "It was really fun." She smiled thoughtfully. She'd promised Mouse she would go back soon, but she couldn't get all the way to Blossom Farm on her own. She'd just have to put up with Kitty calling all the animals zebras. "Mum, can we take Kitty to the farm this weekend? You did say you'd take us."

Mum gave her an apologetic look. "It will have to be sometime over the half-term week, Molly. I've got to help your dad at all the clinics this weekend, I'm afraid."

Molly sighed. She supposed she ought to be glad that Dad was a vet – she'd met most of the animals she loved because they came to the surgery, after all – but sometimes she wished he and Mum weren't quite so busy.

"Perhaps later on next week," Mum promised. "Wednesday or Thursday."

Molly nodded, but inside she was thinking that Wednesday was five whole days away – and she had promised Mouse she'd be back really soon!

She had to find another way to get back to the farm.

Chapter Four

The Missing Piglet

"Oh dear, really? Mmm. Well, I'll be there later on this morning, Mrs Gordon. Yes, see you later."

"Another call-out?" Mum said sympathetically, handing Dad a piece of toast and marmalade to gulp down before he rushed back to the surgery.

It might be Saturday morning, but busy vets didn't get much of a rest at the weekend, even when it was half-term. Molly was still in her pyjamas,

and Dad had already been on one
emergency call.

"All the way over to North Green!"
Dad sighed and took a huge bite of toast.

Molly pricked up her ears. "North
Green?" That was where Blossom Farm
was.

"Yup, that new farm. They've got a
lame horse. It's where you went yesterday,
wasn't it, Moll?"

Molly stared at him, wondering how

she could have missed that. "I didn't know you were the vet for Blossom Farm!"

"Well, I've only been there once," Dad pointed out. "They've been very lucky so far; they look after those animals so well, they haven't needed me."

Molly nodded. "They did all look very happy," she agreed. Except for poor little Mouse. "So, are you going out there today?" she asked, crossing her fingers under the table.

"Mm-hm." Dad had shoved the rest of the toast in his mouth in one go, ignoring Mum's disapproving look. "Want to come?"

Molly beamed at him. "Yes, please!"

"I'd go and change out of your pyjamas, then," Dad suggested, grinning.

★

Molly went straight to find Mouse, but when she reached his little pen, she pulled up short, staring in surprise. Instead of dainty little Mouse, there was a great big ginger-and-black pig, who looked at her hopefully, clearly thinking she might have brought him something to eat.

"Sorry, I haven't got any food," she told him, and the pig, although not magical like Mouse, clearly understood her well enough. He gave a loud and disgusted snort, and went to lie down in one of those mud puddles that Mouse had picked his way around so carefully.

Molly turned round worriedly and saw the same girl she'd spoken to the day before. "Excuse me," she called. "Where's the little pig? Mouse?"

"Oh! I'm afraid he's going to be sold," the girl told her.

"Why?" Molly whispered in horror.

"Well, he's so shy, and he was obviously getting upset whenever people tried to stroke him. We just thought he'd be better off on a normal farm, without visitors."

Molly nodded. It did make sense. "So, he's gone?" she asked sadly. She was too late.

"No, we've just moved him out of the public pens for the moment," the girl explained. "He's over in the part we keep for animals who aren't very well. That stable block over there."

Molly nodded. It was actually where

her dad had gone to look at the lame horse.

"But he's OK, isn't he?" she murmured.

"He's fine," the girl assured her. "But just as shy as ever, I'm afraid."

Molly nodded. She was really hoping she could do something about that. "Thank you!" she told the girl, and hurried over to the stable block.

Her dad gave her a quick wave and went back to examining the horse's foot, and Molly quickly searched the pens for Mouse – or rather, she looked for a pen that seemed to be empty, but had that faint fizz of magic.

It was a little one, down at the end of the building, with a sort of wooden crate for a sleeping shelter. It was nice of the farm people to give Mouse that stall, Molly thought, with somewhere he could easily hide away. It was clear that they only wanted him to be happy.

"Mouse!" she whispered, and this time the piglet popped out of his hiding place much more quickly and pattered over to her to be petted and stroked.

"You came back!" he said delightedly, speaking out loud this time, as there was only Molly's dad around to hear, and he was up at the other end of the stables. "Oh, I hoped you would." Then he looked around sadly. "They've moved me, because I'm useless, you see."

"Don't you like it here?" Molly asked in surprise. "It's much quieter. There aren't any children calling and trying to see what's in your pen. I would have thought it would be better for you."

Mouse shook his head. "No. They've given up on me now. I'm to be sold, did you know?"

"One of the girls told me, when I asked where you were," Molly admitted sadly.

"I'm no use as a children's farm animal." Mouse rested his chin sadly on the rails of his stall.

"Do you want to be, then?" Molly asked, feeling rather confused.

"Of course!" Mouse stared at her in surprise. "Who wouldn't want to? Being stroked and petted and loved all day? And I like children, very much." He sighed, and his ears flopped down. "I'm just too shy to let them see it, that's all. Children are so noisy and quick and scrabbly. Molly, if the farm sells me, I shall probably have to go and live in a horrible muddy field, and I hate mud! Really, I can't stand it. I like being clean. You have to help me!"

"I will, I promise I will," Molly told him, patting his head lovingly. "Only ... I don't quite see what I can do..."

"Couldn't you do something magic?" Mouse asked hopefully. "I can feel the magic inside you, I'm sure you could."

Molly gave a doubtful little nod. "I can try..." She had thought about an anti-shyness spell herself, after all. It was just that she had no idea how to make one. When she had done spells before, someone had almost always helped her, like Silver the unicorn had. "Do you know anything about spells?" she asked Mouse hopefully.

The little pig shook his head. "Not the least thing, I'm afraid. But I'm good at cheering people up," he added, seeing Molly's downcast face. He rubbed his little pink snout against her cheek and blew lovingly in her ear.

Molly jumped as a rush of sudden happiness ran through her, a certainty that she *would* find some way to help Mouse, if only she tried.

"Wow!" she murmured, looking down

at the piglet. "How did you do that?"

Mouse shrugged. "That's what I do," he explained. "That's my magic."

Molly stared at him thoughtfully. "We have to stop you being shy," she said firmly. "It would be an awful waste if you ended up living in the middle of a field. Think how many people you could cheer up if only they could pat you!" She nodded determinedly to herself. "I'll find a spell somehow."

Mouse jumped, all four trotters off the ground at once in his excitement. "Thank you, Molly! I'm so glad I met you that day. And the boy too – it was such a good day."

"The boy?" Molly asked in surprise. Who did Mouse mean?

"Yes, the boy who was talking to me just before you came." Mouse nodded. "He wasn't quite like you; I don't think he could really hear me, not the way you can. But he was definitely special."

"That was Ben, from my school. I

made him go away, because he was poking you with that stick – or at least it looked like he was." Molly frowned worriedly. Had she really been unfair to Ben?

Mouse sighed. "That was only because he wanted me to come out. He shouldn't have tried to make me, but he didn't mean any harm. He was sad; he wanted to stroke me. Anyway, I should like to see him again; he was only trying to help, and I think he needed cheering up too. Oh, shh, they're coming!" And he skittered quickly back into his box.

Molly turned round to see her dad and Mrs Gordon, the owner of the farm, coming towards her.

"Time to go, Molly!" her dad called. "Who've you been chatting to?" He smiled at Mrs Gordon. "Sometimes I really do think that Molly can talk to animals."

Molly smiled back shyly. "A little pig…"

"Oh! Mouse?" Mrs Gordon looked surprised. "You must have a gift with animals, Molly; he's the shyest little thing we've ever seen."

Molly looked back at the box, and called Mouse in her head. *Mouse, it's only one person, Mrs Gordon — she's nice! Couldn't you come and see her? If you show her you can be friendly after all, maybe they'll change their minds about selling you!*

There was no movement in the stall. *Think of the mud!* Molly hissed silently at Mouse. And a little black trotter appeared at the door of the crate, followed by a tentative pink snout. Slowly, reluctantly, Mouse crept out of his hiding place, and came step by slow step across the stall.

"Goodness, he's coming to say hello!"
Mrs Gordon whispered, holding out a
gentle hand. "What a little dear," she
added, as Mouse allowed her to stroke all
round his ears. He glanced anxiously up
at Molly, and she could see that he was
shivering very slightly.

"Perhaps we've been wrong," Mrs
Gordon murmured. "We were going to
sell him, you see. Being out in the main
part of the farm seemed to upset him,

and it wasn't fair. But you'd never think that now."

Closing his eyes slightly, Mouse nuzzled against her hand, and Molly whispered silently, *Well done, Mouse!*

But when Mrs Gordon stood up and led Molly and her dad back to the entrance of the stables, Molly looked back, about to tell Mouse that maybe he didn't need a spell after all.

He hadn't even bolted back to his box to recover, she realized sadly. He was so frightened that he'd just dived under a pile of straw to hide. She could see it shaking, and one polished trotter was sticking out.

"I'll come back," she whisper-promised. "With the spell. Soon."

Chapter Five

The Magic Turnip

It was all very well to say she'd be back
with the spell, Molly thought to herself
sadly as she peeled Kitty a banana, but
she had no idea how to make it. Mum
was desperately trying to do some
paperwork for the surgery and had put
a DVD on for Molly and Kitty, but
Kitty kept wanting snacks, and drinks,
and didn't like the DVD after all. Molly
couldn't concentrate on the film anyway.
She kept worrying about Mouse. It was

now Sunday afternoon. She'd promised him a spell. What was she going to do?

"Don't want this DVD," Kitty whined. "Play with me, Molly!" Molly sighed and switched the television off.

"What do you want to play?" she asked, expecting that it would be dolls, but Kitty was already running to the toy cupboard and hauling out a box of pretend food.

"Café!" she said, happily flinging the food out of the box.

Molly made an "oh no" face behind Kitty's back. She knew how long Kitty could play this game for. But after about twenty minutes of ordering cups of tea from Kitty the waitress, Mum came back into the living room.

"Oh, Molly, thank you, that was so helpful. I've got it all done." She gave Molly a big grateful hug. "I'm sorry Dad

and I've been
so busy lately.
You definitely
need a reward
for helping. I'm
not working on
Wednesday –
would you like
it if we went
to the cinema?
We could take
Alice with us
too."

Molly hugged her back hard. This was
her chance to get back and see Mouse!
"That would be great, but actually, Mum,
could we go to Blossom Farm again
instead? Kitty hasn't been there yet, and I
really loved it. I bet Kitty would too."

Mum nodded. "Well, it must have been

good. If you're sure, that's fine. Do you want to take Alice with us? Shall I ring her mum?"

Molly was just about to say yes when a little smile curled up her mouth at the corners. Of course! It was perfect! Mouse had said that he wanted to see Ben again. "Can we ask Ben instead?"

Her mum looked blank. "What, not Alice? Do I know Ben?"

"Ben Winters. The one who broke his arm last term. You know."

"Oh!" Mum looked surprised. "I thought you couldn't stand Ben Winters. Isn't he the one who was so mean to Alice?"

Molly chewed her lip a little. "Ye-es," she admitted. "But actually I think he might not be that bad. I think he's shy too, and he was being mean to cover it up." Molly really hoped she was right about this. But she trusted Mouse – he had obviously seen something special about Ben, even if Molly couldn't tell what it was.

"Well, if you think so," Mum said, a little doubtfully. "Do you want to phone him?"

Molly nodded. They had a list of everyone's phone numbers from their class pinned up on the kitchen notice board. She tapped out Ben's number, wondering quite what she was going to say.

Luckily, it was Ben who answered. "Hello?"

"Um, Ben? It's Molly. From school."

"Oh. Right." Ben sounded confused.

"Do you want to come on another trip to Blossom Farm with me and my sister?" Molly blurted out. "On Wednesday? My mum's taking us for a treat."

There was silence for a moment. "Me?" Ben asked. "Are you sure?"

Molly rolled her eyes. "I wouldn't be asking if I wasn't..." But she could see why Ben was confused. She was glad when he said, "I mean, yes, sorry. Please."

"Er... Great. Can my mum talk to your mum then? About dropping you off and stuff?"

Molly handed the phone over to her mum, feeling relieved. She was almost sure she was doing a good thing, but only almost. She just hoped Ben was going to behave himself.

Now that she had two problems solved, Molly was free to go back to worrying about the spell for Mouse. The thing was, she had no idea how to start making a spell, even though she'd spent what seemed like days and days thinking about it, and trying to write spells in her notebook. She just couldn't seem to make them real. The only spell she had made up herself before had just turned up in her mind when she needed it; she hadn't planned it at all.

She needed help.

So when Grandad arrived to look after them on Tuesday, Molly persuaded him and Kitty that what they really wanted to do on a beautiful autumn day was go to Larkfield Wood and kick leaves about (for Kitty), and look for mushrooms (for Grandad).

And then perhaps they would have a quick game of hide and seek, and Molly would have the chance to slip off and find the cottage over the stream. She had been so frightened of it once, when she had heard that a witch lived there, but she had met the witch now, and her gorgeous grey kitten, Sparkle. Surely they would be just the people to ask about a spell?

It was fun, tramping through the leaves, even though that wasn't actually why Molly had wanted to come. She and Kitty had their wellies on, and when they got to the stream, Molly suggested they try making stick boats. Grandad was sitting on an old tree stump, looking a bit puffed.

"I'm just going that way to look for some bigger sticks, OK, Grandad?" Molly asked, jumping to the other side of the stream.

Grandad nodded, mopping his forehead with a handkerchief. "Don't go too far, Molly," he warned her.

"I won't," Molly promised. It was true, after all. The cottage really wasn't far, she was sure.

She couldn't see it, though. She couldn't even find the pretty clearing where she'd played with Sparkle. The wood looked different with its autumn colours; it was all very confusing. At last Molly pulled out the locket with Sparkle's whisker tucked inside it. The witch had given it to her as a magical way to call if she needed help, and she had never used it. Molly gripped it tightly and whispered, "Please come..."

But no one did.

Molly went to bed that night convinced that she was far too worried to sleep. Mum had promised to take them all to the farm the next day, and she still hadn't any way to help Mouse. But it seemed that worrying had worn her out. She woke up in the middle of the night, slightly surprised that she had ever gone to sleep.

She realized it was an idea that had woken her. *Maybe Sparkle and the witch hadn't come because she didn't really need them?* The locket was only for emergencies, after all.

Molly sat up, hugging her knees thoughtfully. But she *did* need a spell.

Mouse needed it desperately, or he was going to be sold.

Unless... Did he actually need a spell? Molly had never been a shy person, and she loved talking to people, so it was quite hard for her to understand how he felt, but would an imaginary spell be just as good for Mouse? Something that she could give him that would make him think he'd been cured? Smiling to herself, Molly lay back down against her pillow. It was sneaky, but it was clever...

The next morning, Molly waited until no one was looking and took a turnip out of the basket where Mum kept all the vegetables. She was sure Mum wouldn't mind – there were loads in there, and Molly hated turnips, so the fewer Mum was able to put in the stew she was going to make for tea, the better, as far as Molly was concerned. And she was sure a pig would love one. There were signs up at the farm asking visitors not to feed the animals except on the special food the farm gave out, but Molly was certain that one extra turnip wouldn't hurt Mouse.

Molly's nana had given her a box of special cake decorating ingredients; food colouring, icing pens, sprinkles, and the best bit, edible glitter. Molly wasn't really supposed to use them in her bedroom but if she was careful, Mum would never know. She whisked the box upstairs after breakfast, and set to work making the turnip look magical. It wasn't easy. Somehow, turnips just looked like turnips, even if you painted them pink with food colouring, and scattered them with golden glitter, and stuck on candy stars with an icing pen.

"Perhaps a pig would think that looks good," Molly sighed to herself at last. "Oh, I really hope this works!" She wrapped the turnip up in tissue paper and stowed it away inside her little rucksack, and then ran downstairs. It was a only a few minutes to ten, when Ben's mum was due to drop him at Molly's house.

"They're here, Molly!" her mum called, as she came into the kitchen. "Oh, there you are. I think this must be Ben's mum's car just driving up."

Molly went to open the door, crossing her fingers inside her pocket. She really hoped that this was going to work...

Chapter Six

Turnip Time!

"I want to go with Ben," Kitty said firmly, and everyone stared at her in surprise. She took Ben's hand and pulled him towards a pen of lion-head rabbits. "Come and see the bunnies, Ben."

"Wow," Molly muttered to herself. "Maybe Mouse was right and he isn't that bad, if Kitty likes him. And he's being nice back!"

It was true. Ben was crouching down by the pen with Kitty, showing her which

rabbit was which from the board tied on
to the wire.

"What a nice boy," Molly's mum
commented. "I'm so glad you're friends
with him now, Molly. I remember Bella's
mum telling me his parents split up last
year. It must have been very hard for
him."

Molly gave her a surprised glance.

Molly hadn't known that. Perhaps it explained why Ben was so horrible sometimes.

"Molly, will you be all right if I just nip to the loo?" Mum asked. "It's just there. I won't be long."

Molly was just going to join Kitty and Ben by the rabbits when she saw another boy from school, Josh. He was one of the boys who sometimes hung around with Ben, and he could be pretty mean too.

Josh came up behind Ben and tapped him on the shoulder, and as Molly hurried forward she heard him say, "Got a new best friend?" as he smirked at Kitty.

"Don't be stupid," Ben muttered.

Josh saw Molly and laughed. "You're here with *her*? Turning into a girl, Ben?"

"Shut up, Josh!" Molly said scornfully, but Ben had gone red. He stood up quickly, as though he was going to yell at Josh.

"Don't go, I want to look at the bunnies more!" Kitty wailed, grabbing at his jacket.

"Ohhh, she wants to look at the *bunnies*!" Josh teased.

Ben pulled sharply away from Kitty, accidentally pulling her over, and ran off, shoving Josh as he went.

Josh took one look at Kitty, wailing on the floor, muttered a quick, "Sorry!" and dashed away too before he got into trouble.

"I can't believe Ben did that!" Molly said angrily as she helped Kitty up.

"What happened to Kitty? And where's Ben?" asked Mum, coming back from the loo at just the wrong time.

"Um, Ben saw a friend... He'll be back in a minute. And Kitty just slipped," Molly said quickly, grabbing a jelly bean she happened to have in her pocket and stuffing it into Kitty's mouth. "Mum, she wants to stay and look at the rabbits. Can I go and see the horses? I know where everything is. And I'll find Ben and take him with me."

Mum nodded. "All right. We'll meet you at the play barn in half an hour."

"OK." Molly nodded and headed off, scowling. She was going straight to find Ben. She didn't care if he was shy and miserable, he wasn't going to get away with knocking down her little sister! Molly didn't think he'd hurt Kitty on purpose — it was Josh he'd been angry with — but he should have stopped and said sorry.

"Where would he have gone?" Molly muttered as she searched her way around the different animals. "I can't see him anywhere!"

Then she stopped for a moment. Ben had looked really upset. Perhaps he'd gone off to hide somewhere? Maybe he thought he might cry and he didn't want anyone to see?

Molly frowned. She was still cross with Ben for hurting Kitty, but she was starting to feel worried about him too. She worked her way round the llama enclosure, trying to think of places where someone might hide. Then suddenly she realized the one place she hadn't looked – the pens where the sick animals were. Where Mouse was. Mouse had been sure that Ben was special, and when they came to the farm before he'd known that Mouse was hiding. What if he'd found Mouse again?

Molly turned round and raced back to the stable block. She had to nip in quickly when no one was looking. Inside all was quiet, but she could sense that she wasn't the only person there. As well as the watchful interest from the lame horse and the other creatures, there was a feeling of panicked worry in the air.

Ben!

He was curled up in the corner at the back of the barn, right next to Mouse's pen. And, amazingly enough, Mouse was with him, his snout poked through the bars to nuzzle Ben lovingly.

Is he all right? Molly asked Mouse.

Hello, Molly. No, he's very sad about something. I'm trying to help, but it's hard work.

Molly frowned. Poor Ben. She didn't

feel angry with him any more, now that she could see him slumped in the corner like that.

He looked up at her as she came closer. "Sorry I pushed your sister," he muttered.

"You didn't mean to," Molly said, crouching down beside him. "Josh Baynes is a total pig." *Sorry!* she added to Mouse, giving him an apologetic look.

What is the matter with him? Mouse asked Molly.

Molly frowned. *I think he's shy like you. Another boy from our school was mean to him just now.*

He's shy? Mouse sounded very surprised. *Can children be shy? He was very noisy before when he was trying to get me to come out and see him. How strange.*

It is, isn't it? Do you think you can cheer him up with your magic? Would it help if he

71

was holding you?

Mouse looked thoughtful. *Have you brought the spell you've made for me? Could you use it on both of us?*

Molly went pink. *I don't think he would like it very much. It's a spell in a turnip.*

Oooh, turnips are my favourite. You are clever! Mouse told her admiringly. *Well, perhaps if I eat it while he's holding me, it will work for him too.*

Molly nodded, feeling ashamed. She was sure it wouldn't work at all. Oh, why hadn't she tried harder to make a real spell? But there was nothing she could do about it now.

"I brought a treat for Mouse," she told Ben. "Shall we get him out?"

"We can't!" Ben's face was shocked.

Molly shrugged. "No one's here to see. And if we're caught in here we'll be in trouble anyway, so we might as well."

Ben looked doubtful, but he nodded.
"I'd really like to hold him. There's
something special about him; I don't
know what it is."

Yes, yes, lift me out, Mouse agreed. *Let
him cuddle me.*

Molly reached down into the pen and
picked Mouse up. He was surprisingly
heavy for someone so small. She passed
him gently to Ben and watched him
snuggle into Ben's arms. Ben even smiled.

Molly reached into her rucksack and unwrapped the turnip. Ben gave her a funny look when he saw the glitter and candy stars, but she glared back and he didn't say anything.

Ooh, gosh, that even looks magical! Mouse cried happily. *Is it really for me?*

Molly nodded. *All for you. I just hope it works.*

I can tell that it will, Mouse said, sounding very confident. *It looks so special. You're very clever, Molly.*

Molly felt worse and worse. She hadn't realized when she came up with the fake-spell plan that it would make her feel so guilty, and that she'd have to lie to Mouse. But it was all to help him! Hopefully that didn't make it so bad? She held the turnip out and watched Mouse take it delicately, closing his eyes as he crunched the delicious treat.

"Mmmph!" he mumbled. *Oh, Molly, this is so yummy! And I can feel the magic working!*

And as Molly watched in amazement, she saw the pink sparkles from the turnip spreading on to Mouse's pink muzzle. She hadn't put that much edible glitter on, had she? No, she surely hadn't. There was a cloud of it now, with here and there a little rainbow star, just like the candy ones she had sprinkled on.

Her fake spell was *working*!

It was shimmering around Ben now too, and he was shaking his head, looking confused, as though he could feel something weird.

"What's happening?" he muttered, and then he smiled, rubbing his cheek against Mouse's ears. "You're one special pig."

He was right, Molly thought. It had to be Mouse's own magic that was working with all the worry and wishing she'd put into the turnip. And the spell had wrapped itself around Ben too!

Oh, Molly. That was a wonderful spell, Mouse said at last, when the pink glittery cloud had died away. *Ben feels all different now. Like he's melted inside.* Then his ears pricked up. *Someone's coming!*

Molly jumped up, and Ben heard the door opening too, and quickly popped

Mouse back into his pen.

"Molly! Here you are!" It was Mum, and she didn't look happy. "You were supposed to meet us at the play barn ages ago!"

Mrs Gordon from the farm was behind Mum and Kitty.

"Oh, it's you, Molly. You aren't really supposed to be in here, you know," she said, sounding rather annoyed.

"I just wanted to see Mouse again," Molly said apologetically. "To see if he'd been getting better. He's being really friendly, Mrs Gordon. I think he's recovered from whatever was wrong with him."

Mrs Gordon crouched down by the pen, looking at Mouse, and he rubbed his snout against her hand, and then stood up against the bars to blow in her face. He winked at Molly as he did it.

"Oh!" Mrs Gordon rubbed her hand

over her face, looking confused. "Yes.
Very friendly. I don't think he needs to
be in here at all." She looked at him
thoughtfully. "And so clean! I wonder
if he'd like to be bathed, as one of the
things we do with the school groups..."

Mouse gave an excited little squeal, and Mrs Gordon laughed. "It's almost as if he heard me!"

Molly smiled, and saw Ben smile too. "It is, isn't it?"

"Hi, Molly! Hi, Alice!" Ben waved as he walked through the school gate, and Alice stared after him in surprise.

"He sounded pleased to see us... I thought he didn't like me at all!" she whispered to Molly.

Molly smiled. "I don't think he's really that bad. I saw him when Mum took me and Kitty back to Blossom Farm. We went round the animals together. He was nice." She didn't think Alice would understand if she said that Ben had actually gone to the farm with her and Mum and Kitty. It would be very hard to explain without also telling Alice that she'd met a magic piglet.

Molly undid her school bag and pulled out something wrapped in pink tissue paper. "I've brought you a present," she said, hoping that this was going to work.

"Ooh, what is it?" Alice asked. "Thank you, Molly!" She started to unwrap the pink paper, and Molly watched anxiously.

As Alice undid the little parcel, a delicious smell rose out of the paper. Molly had begged Mum to let her and Kitty make fairy cakes as an end-of-the-holidays treat yesterday. They'd turned the cake mixture pink with food colouring, and Molly had drizzled on pink icing and sprinkled this particularly perfect cake with glitter and stars, just like Mouse's magic turnip.

She had thought about Mouse all the time she was doing it – hoping that this would be a *real* fairy cake. A magic spell cake for her best friend, to take away Alice's shyness too.

"It's so pretty..." Alice breathed. "Almost too pretty to eat. But it looks so good..." She broke off a little piece of the icing and smiled as the sweetness melted in her mouth. "Oh, Molly, it's the nicest cake ever." She hugged Molly tightly, and Molly beamed at her. She could see just the tiniest hint of gold, shimmering round Alice's dark curly hair.

It might take a while, but she was sure her spell was working...

HOLLY WEBB is the author of the bestselling
Lost in the Snow and its sequel, *Lost in the
Storm*, as well as the popular Triplets series.
She has always loved cats and now
owns a very spoilt one.

Read more about Molly's magical adventures!

The girl who talks to animals

Magic Molly

The Witch's Kitten

HOLLY WEBB

The girl who talks to animals

Magic Molly

The Wish Puppy

HOLLY WEBB

The girl who talks to animals

Magic Molly

The Invisible Bunny

HOLLY WEBB

The girl who talks to animals

Magic Molly

The Secret Pony

HOLLY WEBB